MIGHTY MORPHIN POWER RANGERS™

MORPH INTO MATH

Answers begin on page 53.

Cheryl Saban, Editorial Consultant

GOLDEN & DESIGN and A GOLDEN BOOK are registered trademarks of Western Publishing Company, Inc.

A GOLDEN BOOK®
Western Publishing Company, Inc.
Racine, Wisconsin 53404

1

Find 3 rectangles. Color them blue.

Find 4 squares. Color them red.

2

Find 5 circles. Color them yellow.

Find 6 triangles. Color them green.

Circle the one that would come next in each row.

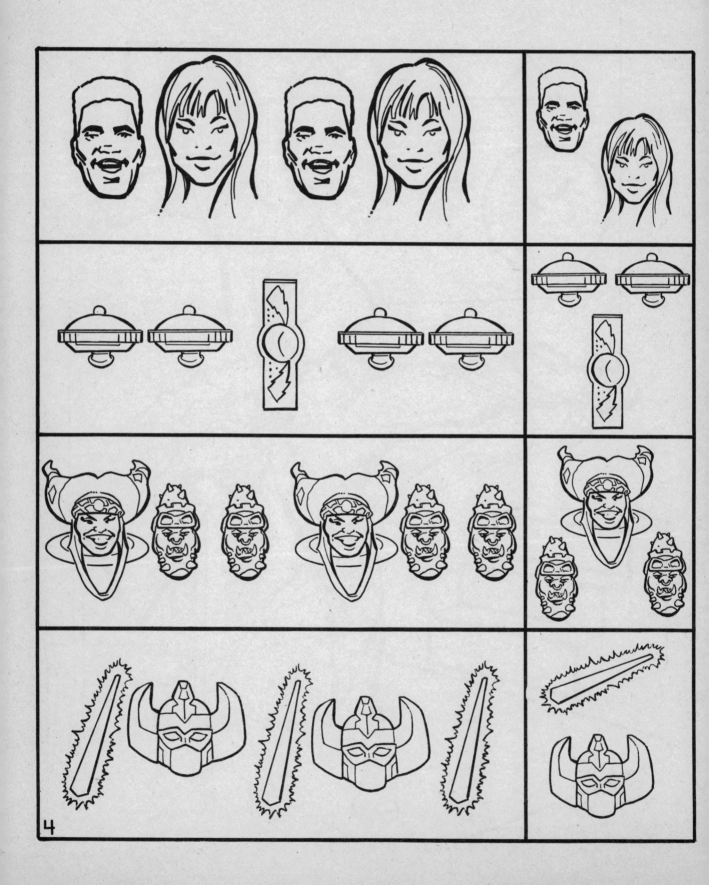

Use a red crayon to lead Jason along the path of triangles to his Power Crystal. Use a yellow crayon to lead Trini along the path of circles to her Power Crystal.

Look at these two pages.
Which bowl has less fruit? Circle it.
Which straw is thicker? Circle it.

Which glass is tallest? Color it orange.
Which spoon is smaller? Color it blue.

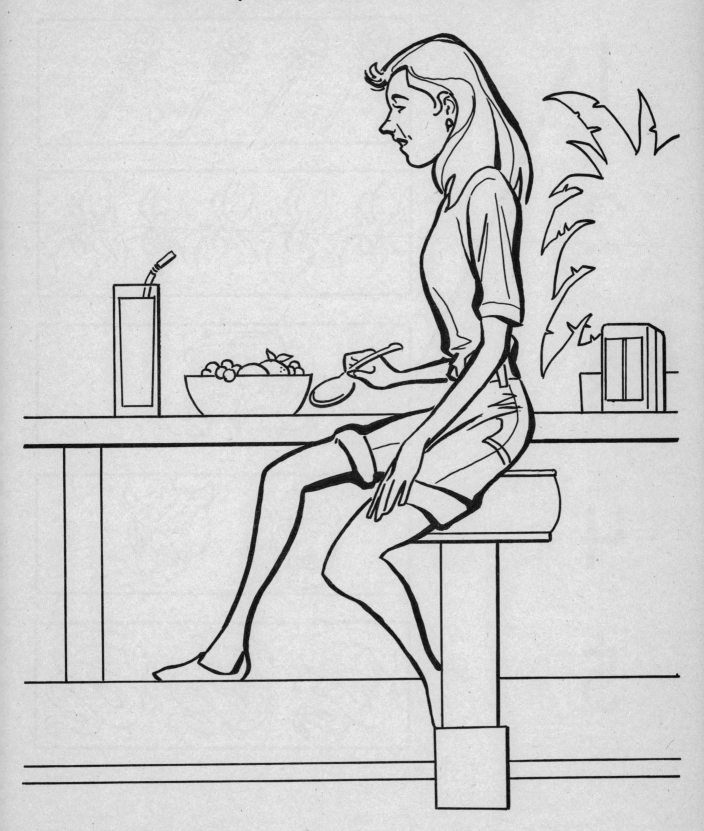

Draw a line from each number
to the group of objects that matches that number.

1

2

3

4

5

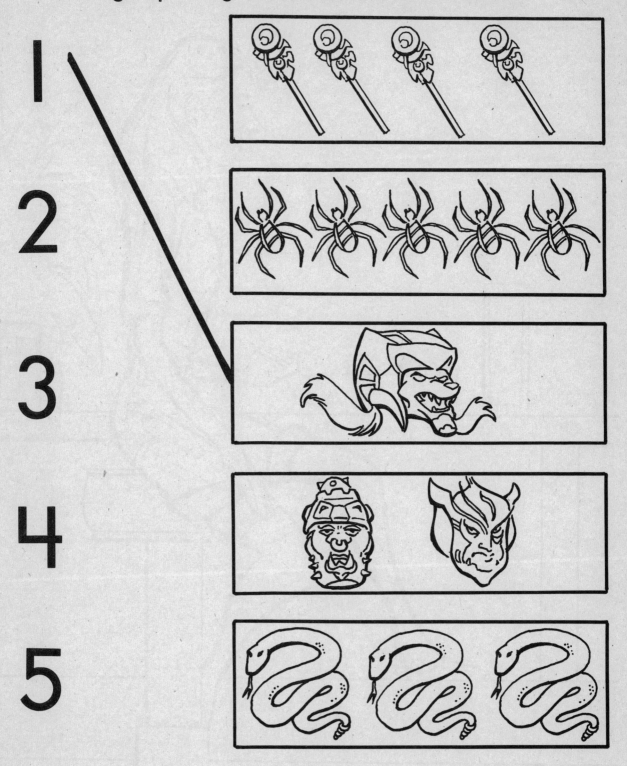

6

7

8

q

10

Find the numbers 1, 2, 3, 4, 5, 6, 7, 8, 9, and 10 hidden in the picture.

What happened first? What happened next?
What happened last? Number the pictures in order.
Write a 1, 2, or 3 in each box.

Connect the dots from 1-10.

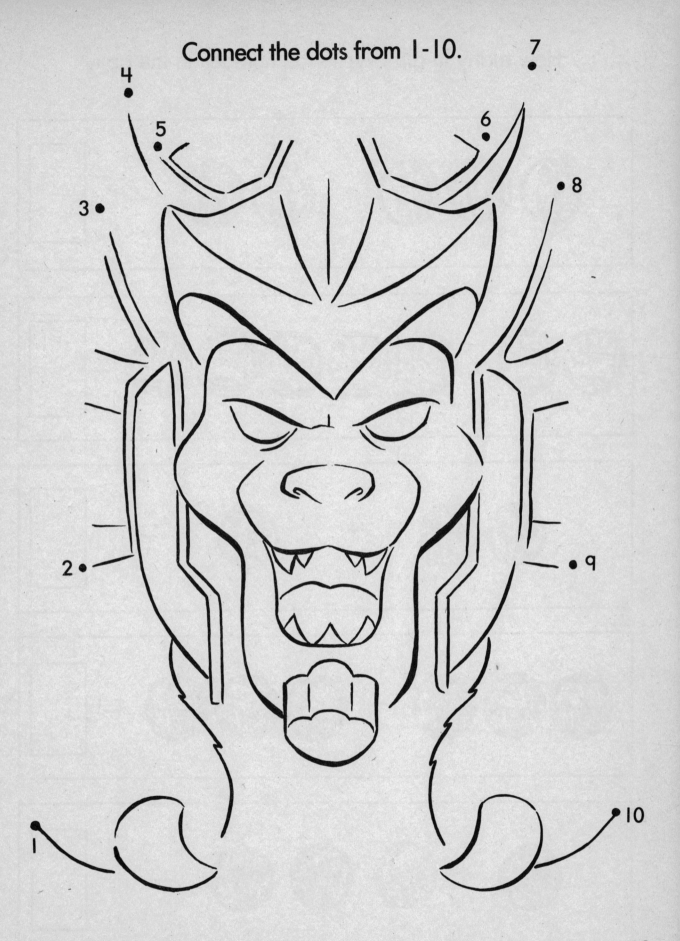

How many in all? Write the number in the box.

What is Billy saying? Add the numbers.
Each answer stands for a letter. Write the letters on the lines.
Read the message.

P
$1 + 1 = \boxed{2}$

R
$2 + 4 = \boxed{6}$

T
$3 + 1 = \boxed{4}$

E
$3 + 2 = \boxed{5}$

S
$6 + 1 = \boxed{7}$

O
$5 + 3 = \boxed{8}$

M
$5 + 4 = \boxed{9}$

L
$8 + 2 = \boxed{10}$

H
$2 + 1 = \boxed{3}$

$$\underset{10}{\text{L}} \ \underset{5}{\text{e}} \ \underset{4}{\text{t}} \text{'} \underset{7}{\text{s}}$$

$$\underset{9}{\text{m}} \ \underset{8}{\text{o}} \ \underset{6}{\text{r}} \ \underset{2}{\text{p}} \ \underset{3}{\text{h}} !$$

15

Jason is meeting Zack after school. Can you help Jason find Zack? Follow the clocks in order from 8:00 to 2:00.

Can you help Jason find a safe path through the Putty Patrollers?
Starting with the first row, lead Jason between two numbers
in each row that add up to 10.

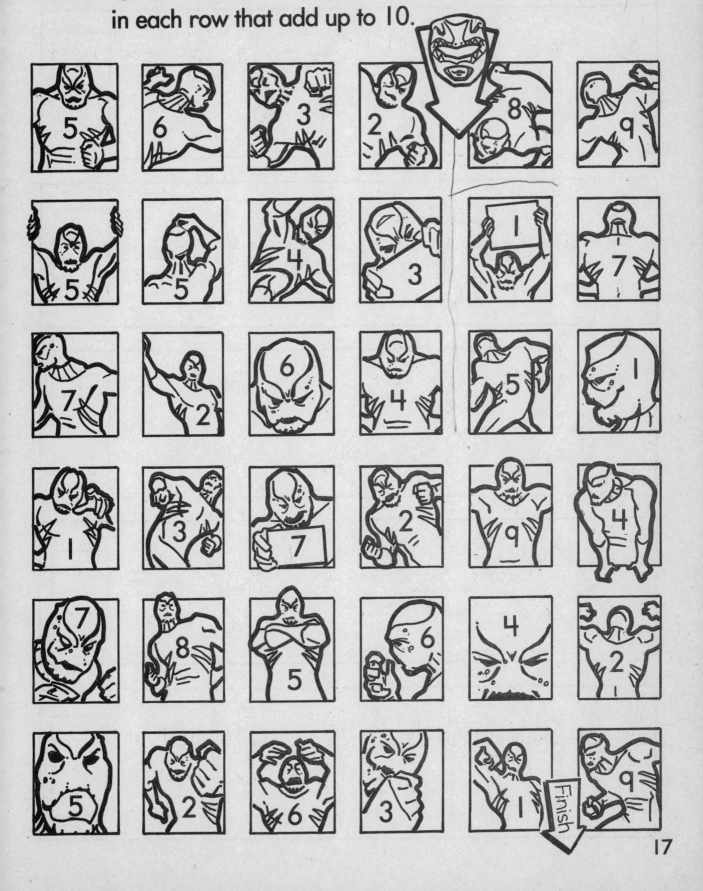

How many are left? Write the number in the box.

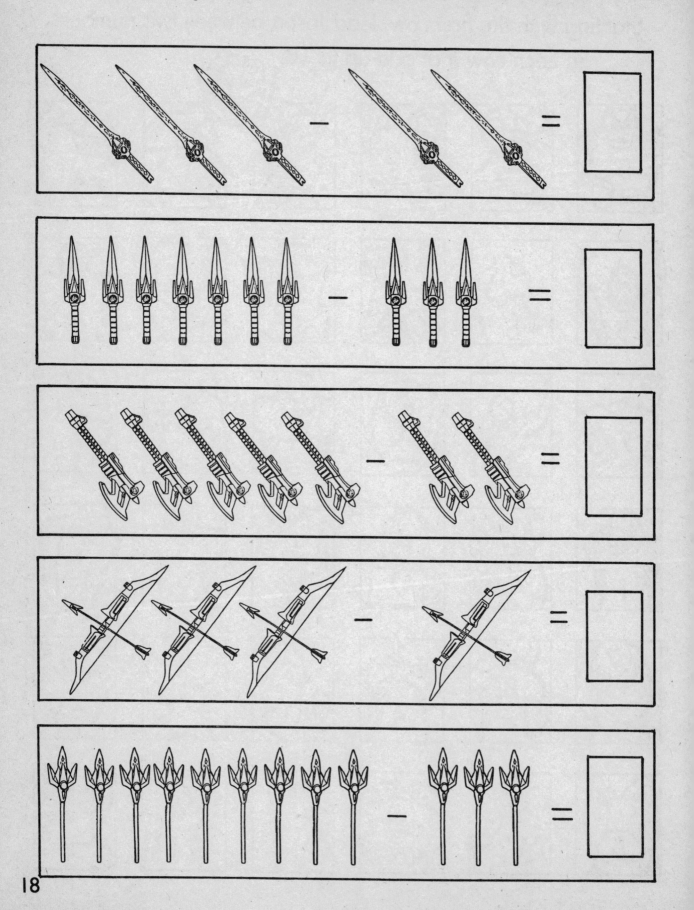

Color all the spaces where the answer is zero.

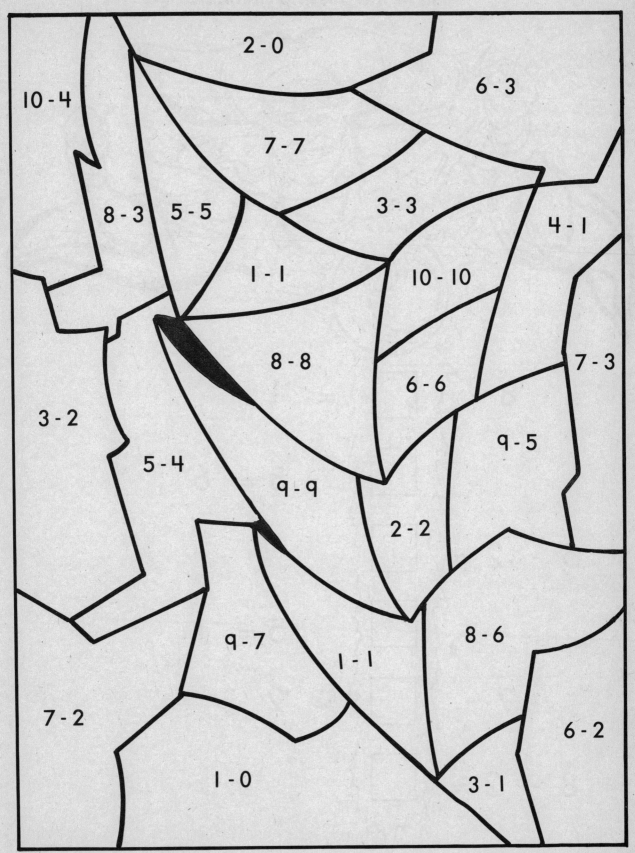

Rita Repulsa made part of each problem disappear!
Fill in the missing numbers.

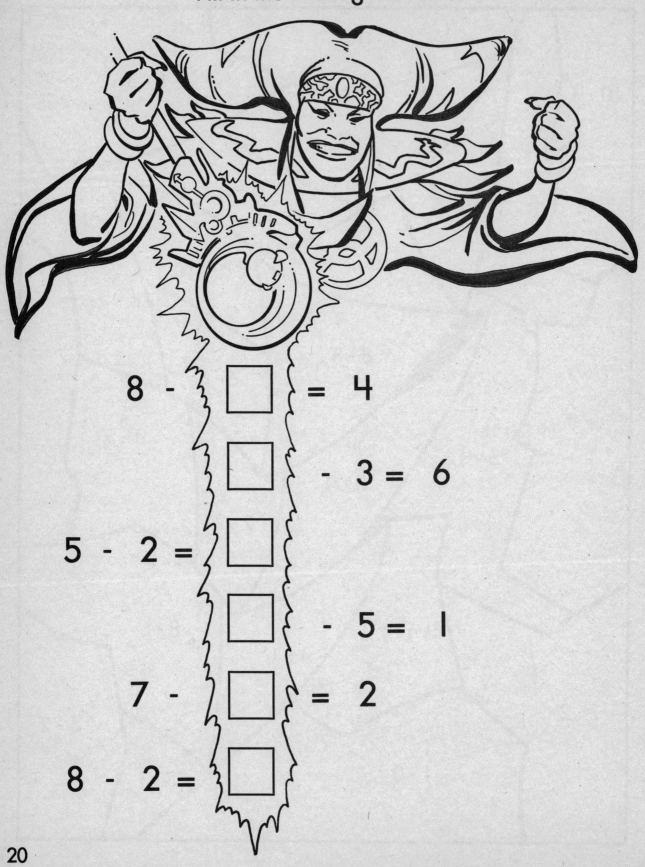

$8 - \boxed{} = 4$

$\boxed{} - 3 = 6$

$5 - 2 = \boxed{}$

$\boxed{} - 5 = 1$

$7 - \boxed{} = 2$

$8 - 2 = \boxed{}$

Color the spaces with answers:
5 Red   7 Yellow
6 Blue   8 Gray

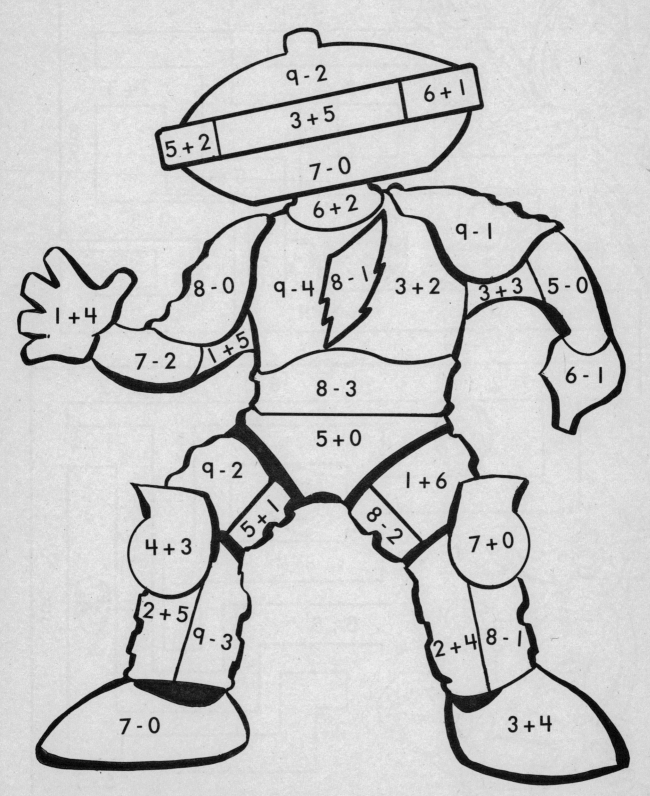

Jason needs Kimberly's help! Can you help her reach Jason in time? Follow the path of facts that equal 5.

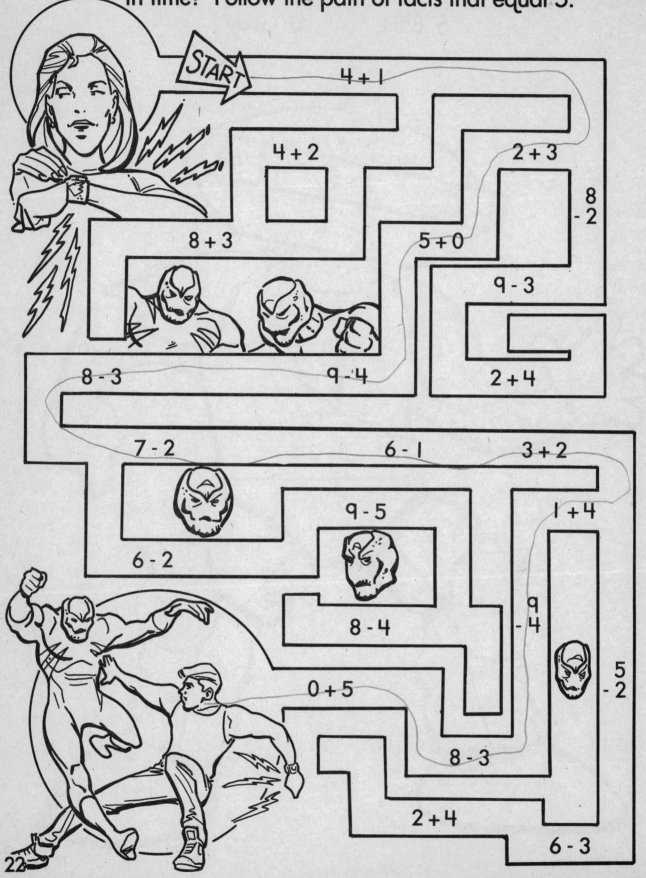

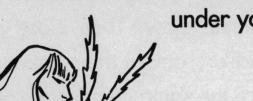

Trini is sending a message to Zack. What is she saying? Add or subtract. Write the letters from the chart under your answers.

1 = Y	5 = E	9 = N
2 = R	6 = H	10 = O
3 = M	7 = T	11 = C
4 = U	8 = A	

8	3	9	4		2	8		6	8
-5	+2	-4	+3		+1	-3		+2	-1
☐	☐	☐	☐		☐	☐		☐	☐

5	9	4		7	6	9	7	8
+2	-3	+1		-6	+4	-5	+0	-2
☐	☐	☐		☐	☐	☐	☐	☐

6	7	8	9	5	9
+5	-2	+1	-2	+0	-7
☐	☐	☐	☐	☐	☐

Play this game with a friend.
Use buttons or coins as playing pieces. Place them on START on the next page. Solve the problems below. Then, close your eyes and put your finger on a square. Look at the number you picked and move your playing piece the same number of spaces. Players take turns. The first player to reach Zordon wins!

$\begin{array}{r} 1 \\ +4 \\ \hline \end{array}$	$\begin{array}{r} 9 \\ -8 \\ \hline \end{array}$	$\begin{array}{r} 3 \\ +3 \\ \hline \end{array}$	$\begin{array}{r} 6 \\ -2 \\ \hline \end{array}$
$\begin{array}{r} 8 \\ -5 \\ \hline \end{array}$	$\begin{array}{r} 2 \\ +3 \\ \hline \end{array}$	$\begin{array}{r} 4 \\ -2 \\ \hline \end{array}$	$\begin{array}{r} 5 \\ +1 \\ \hline \end{array}$
$\begin{array}{r} 2 \\ +2 \\ \hline \end{array}$	$\begin{array}{r} 9 \\ -6 \\ \hline \end{array}$	$\begin{array}{r} 1 \\ +1 \\ \hline \end{array}$	$\begin{array}{r} 7 \\ -6 \\ \hline \end{array}$

START

Putty Patrol Attacks! GO BACK 1

Use Your Power Crystal MORPH AHEAD 3

Battle with Goldar GO BACK 2

FINISH

Write the numbers in order from 1-31 on Trini's calendar.
Color the special dates yellow.

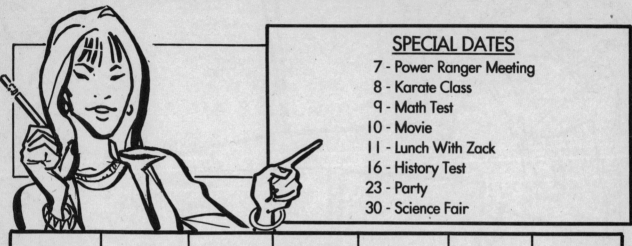

SPECIAL DATES
7 - Power Ranger Meeting
8 - Karate Class
9 - Math Test
10 - Movie
11 - Lunch With Zack
16 - History Test
23 - Party
30 - Science Fair

SUNDAY	MONDAY	TUESDAY	WEDNESDAY	THURSDAY	FRIDAY	SATURDAY
		1				
			31			

Take Alpha Five to the Command Center. Count by 5.

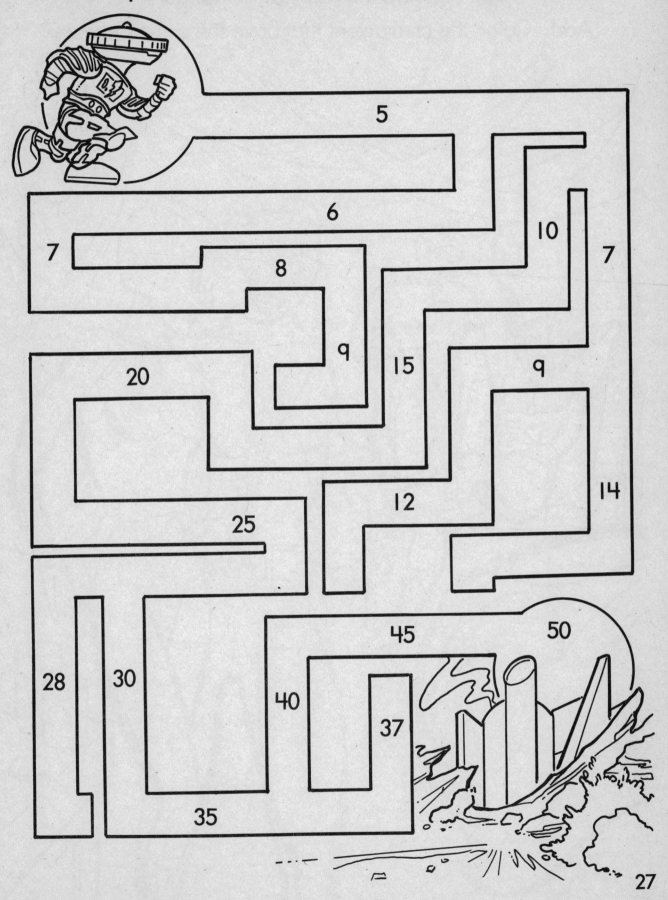

5

6

7

8

10

7

9

15

9

20

25

12

14

45

50

28

30

40

37

35

Can you find the real Power Rangers?
Add. Color the characters that have the same answer.

Zack has a riddle for you! Add the numbers.
Write the letters from the chart under your answers.

11 = B	15 = V	18 = E
12 = T	16 = M	19 = R
13 = U	17 = S	20 = H
14 = N		

7
+5
☐

10
+10
☐

9
+9
☐

13
+1
☐

8
+5
☐

9
+7
☐

6
+5
☐

15
+3
☐

11
+8
☐

12
+5
☐

16
+2
☐

9
+6
☐

10
+8
☐

7
+7
☐

What number is even without the "S"?

30

Can you solve Kimberly's riddle?

Subtract. Write the letters from the chart under your answers.

11 = N	15 = E
12 = O	16 = A
13 = R	17 = S
14 = H	18 = P

$$
\begin{array}{cccccccc}
18 & 19 & 17 & 18 & 18 & 16 & 13 \\
-2 & -1 & -2 & -5 & -1 & -4 & -2 \\
\hline
\square & \square & \square & \square & \square & \square & \square
\end{array}
$$

$$
\begin{array}{cccccccc}
15 & 12 & 19 & 15 & 18 & 17 & 19 & 18 \\
-3 & -1 & -3 & -1 & -6 & -4 & -2 & -3 \\
\hline
\square & \square & \square & \square & \square & \square & \square & \square
\end{array}
$$

What has six legs and two heads?

Have a math race with a friend!
Each player decides which character he or she will be.
One player says, "Ready, Set, GO!" Both players start adding
at the same time. Add 7 to each number in the left-hand column.
The first one has been done for you. The first player to
reach the bottom is the winner!

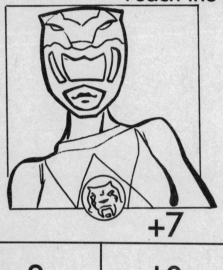

+7

3	10
9	
6	
8	
10	
5	
7	
4	

+7

3	10
9	
6	
8	
10	
5	
7	
4	

Try a race using subtraction.
Subtract 5 from each number in the left-hand column.

-5

16	11
19	
7	
8	
17	
9	
18	
15	

-5

16	11
19	
7	
8	
17	
9	
18	
15	

Subtract. Draw a line from each Power Crystal to its matching Dinozord.

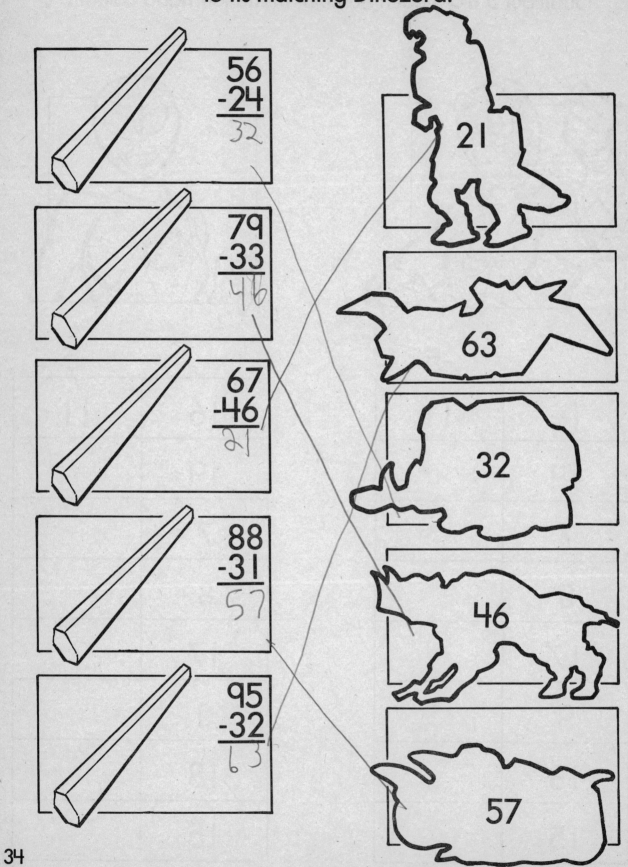

56
-24
32

79
-33
46

67
-46
21

88
-31
57

95
-32
63

21

63

32

46

57

Connect the dots from 1 - 30.

When the Power Rangers are really in trouble, they call on another Ranger for help. Do you know who he is? To find out, cross out each square that has a number you see more than twice. The letters in the remaining squares will spell out the Ranger's name in order from the top.

3 R	7 N	2 A	10 E	4 G	2 A	7 N
2 A	5 T	4 G	3 R	7 N	8 O	10 E
7 N	4 G	10 E	2 A	4 G	3 R	2 A
10 E	3 R	4 G	1 M	2 A	7 N	4 G
4 G	7 N	2 A	3 R	10 E	2 A	3 R
3 R	1 M	4 G	7 N	2 A	6 Y	10 E
2 A	10 E	7 N	4 G	3 R	2 A	4 G

Count by 3 to connect the dots.

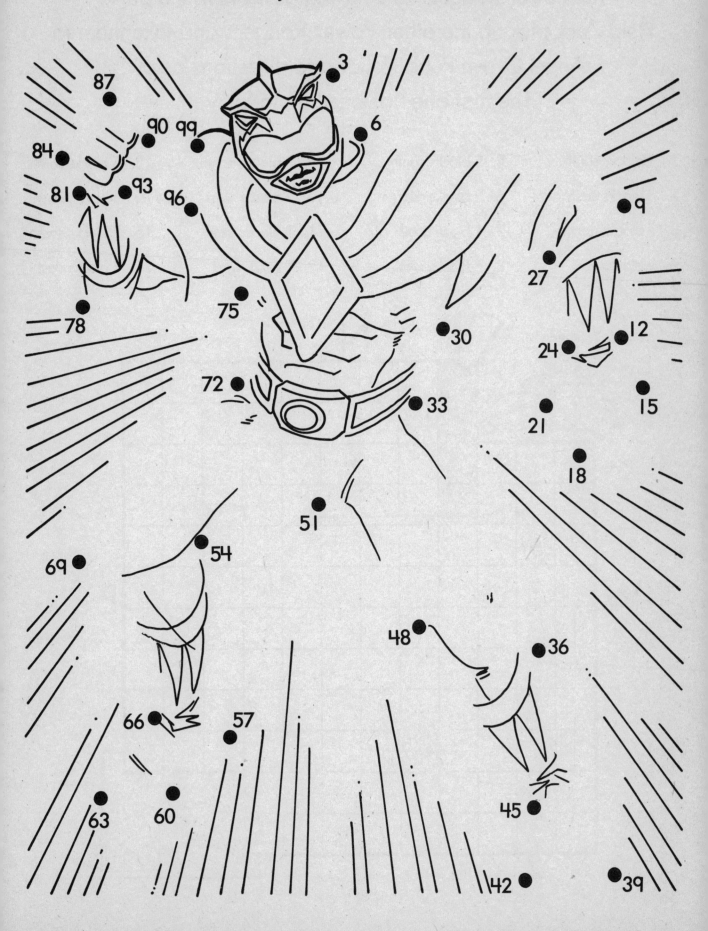

The Power Rangers are having a picnic in the park.
Help Zack pick up the other Power Rangers and take them to
Angel Grove Park. Follow the directions below.
The first one has been done for you.

1. 4 blocks south
2. 3 blocks east
3. 2 blocks north
4. 2 blocks east

5. 5 blocks south
6. 2 blocks east
7. 1 block south
8. 6 blocks west

9. 2 blocks north
10. 3 blocks west
11. 1 block north
12. 1 block west

13. 5 blocks south
14. 4 blocks east
15. 2 blocks south
16. 4 blocks east

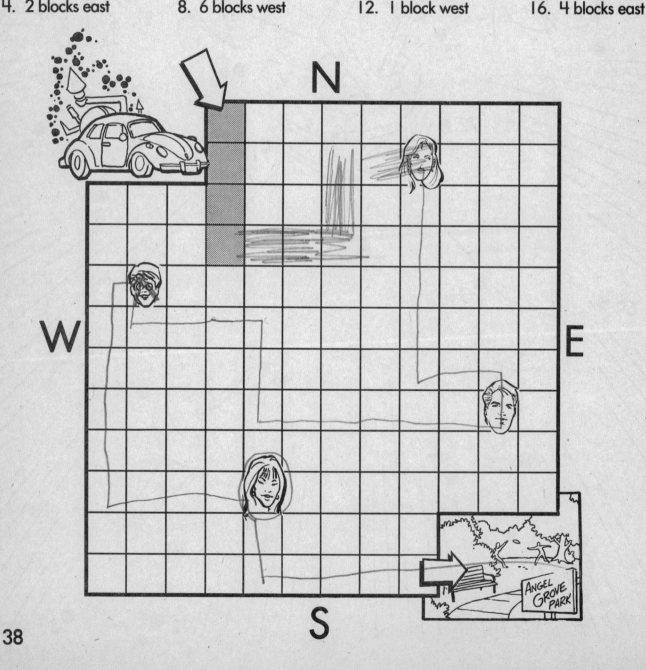

Help the Power Rangers into their cockpits.
Put addition or subtraction signs between the numbers
so that you get the total number shown on each Dinozord.

8	19	5	20	5
[+]	[ ]	[ ]	[ ]	[ ]
7	8	3	9	9
[-]	[ ]	[ ]	[ ]	[ ]
12	6	9	3	13
=	=	=	=	=

5

3

17

14

1

Add or subtract. Use the answers in order (a, b, c, d...) to connect the dots on the next page.

a) 36
+13

b) 23
+52

c) 67
-41

d) 52
+26

e) 35
-22

f) 66
+31

g) 95
-24

h) 87
-46

i) 62
+37

j) 88
-65

k) 32
+12

l) 64
+34

m) 25
+12

n) 66
-21

o) 54
+22

p) 69
-54

q) 36
+21

r) 58
-25

s) 96
-36

t) 75
-54

u) 48
-13

v) 55
+32

w) 25
+13

x) 84
-23

y) 57
-46

z) 77
-23

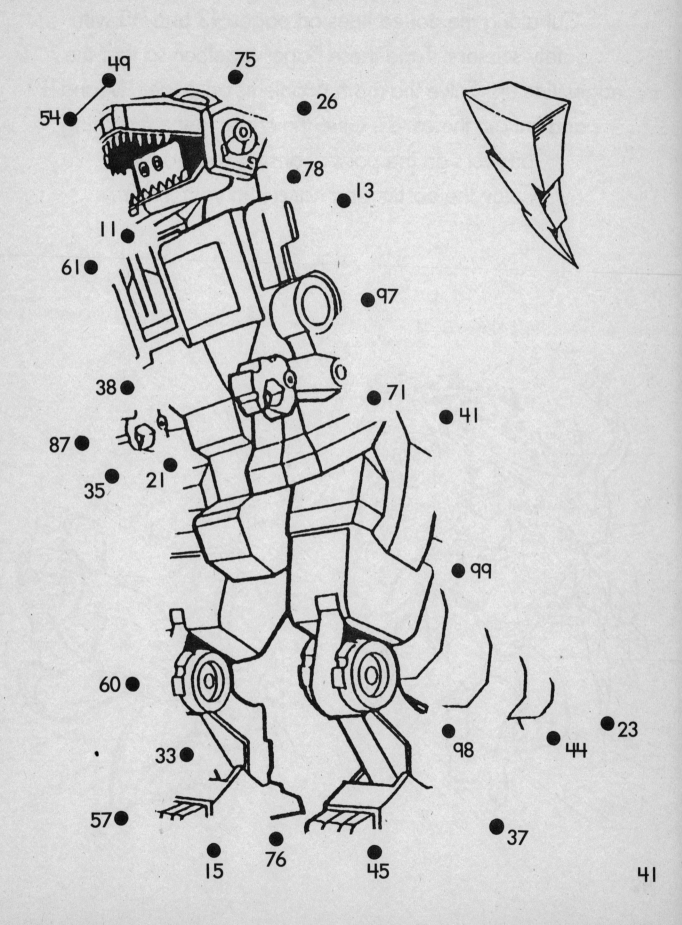

49

75

54

26

78

13

11

61

97

38

71

41

87

21

35

99

60

98 44 23

33

37

57

15 76 45

41

Carefully tear out the next four pages.
Cut along the dotted lines on pages 43 and 45 with
safety scissors. Tape these pages together so that the
edges line up. Solve the math problems on pages 47 and 49
and cut out the cards. Glue the cards to the matching
answers on the poster, answer-side-down.
Color the poster and hang it in your room.

78	33
97	58
45	18
67	11

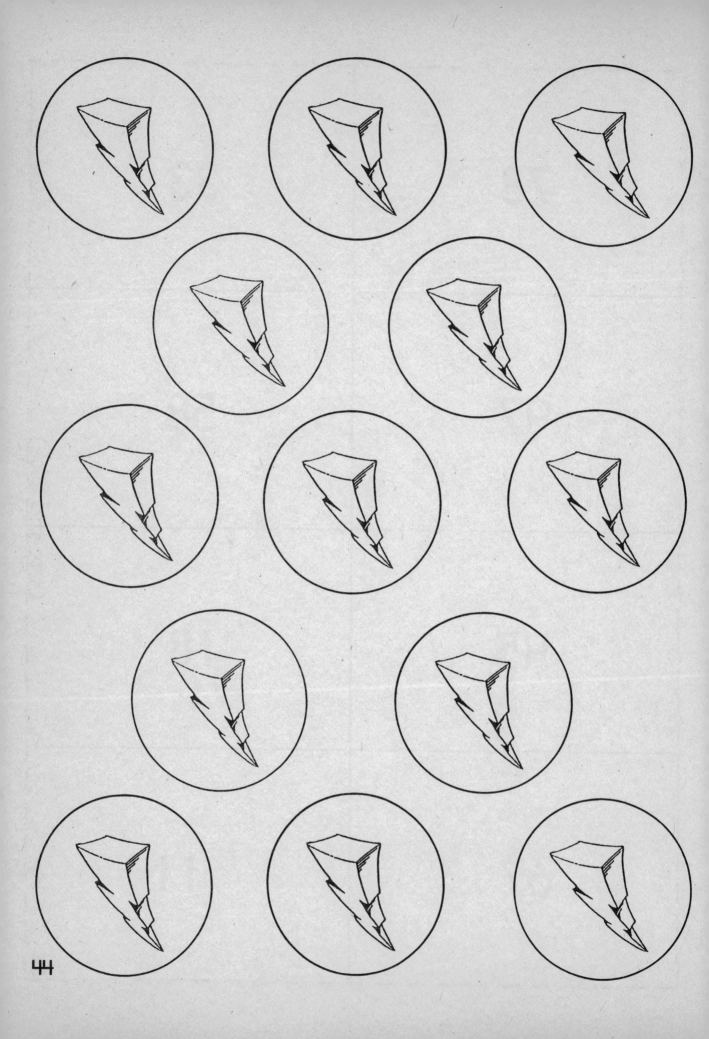

44

39	25
95	72
84	52
66	42

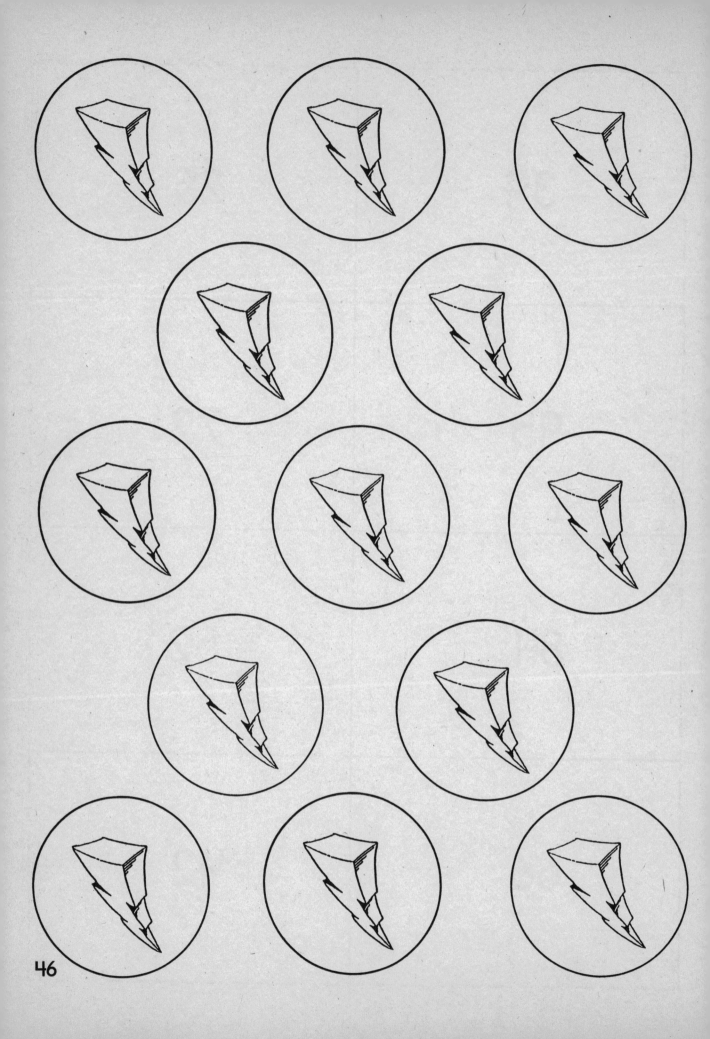

$$\begin{array}{r} 26 \\ +32 \\ \hline \end{array}$$

$$\begin{array}{r} 97 \\ -30 \\ \hline \end{array}$$

$$\begin{array}{r} 87 \\ -76 \\ \hline \end{array}$$

$$\begin{array}{r} 21 \\ +24 \\ \hline \end{array}$$

$$\begin{array}{r} 47 \\ -14 \\ \hline \end{array}$$

$$\begin{array}{r} 15 \\ +82 \\ \hline \end{array}$$

$$\begin{array}{r} 22 \\ +56 \\ \hline \end{array}$$

$$\begin{array}{r} 79 \\ -61 \\ \hline \end{array}$$

$$\begin{array}{r} 34 \\ +32 \\ \hline \end{array}$$

$$\begin{array}{r} 98 \\ -56 \\ \hline \end{array}$$

$$\begin{array}{r} 65 \\ -13 \\ \hline \end{array}$$

$$\begin{array}{r} 24 \\ +15 \\ \hline \end{array}$$

$$\begin{array}{r} 59 \\ -34 \\ \hline \end{array}$$

$$\begin{array}{r} 20 \\ +64 \\ \hline \end{array}$$

$$\begin{array}{r} 44 \\ +51 \\ \hline \end{array}$$

$$\begin{array}{r} 83 \\ -11 \\ \hline \end{array}$$

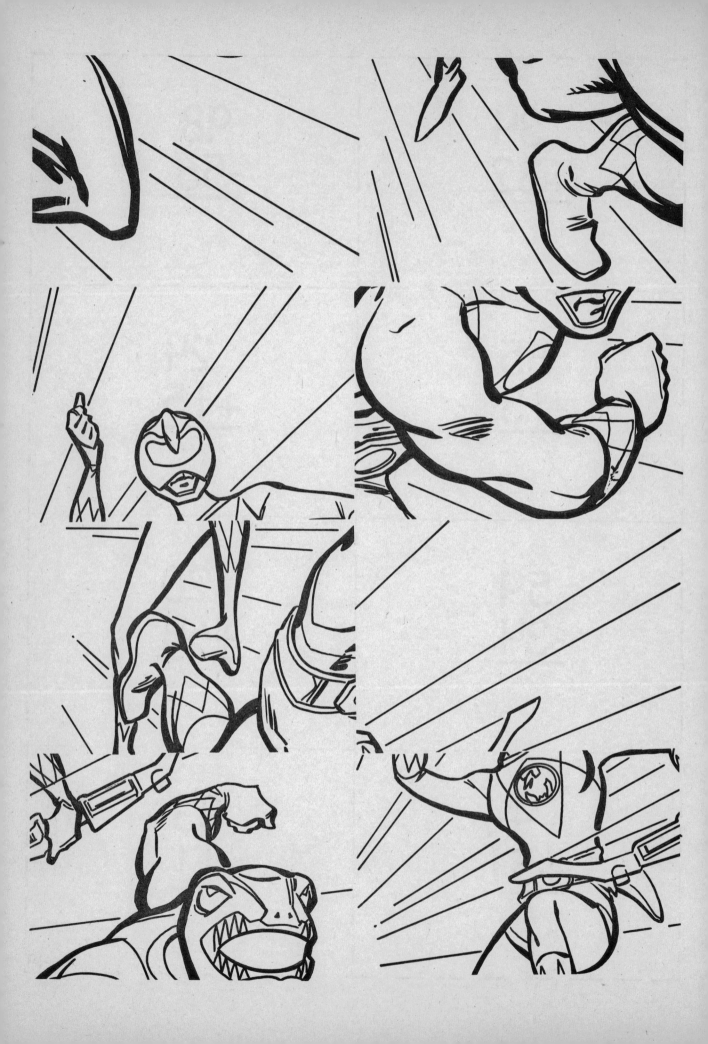

CERTIFICATE

_____

(Write your name)

HAS MORPHED INTO MATH!

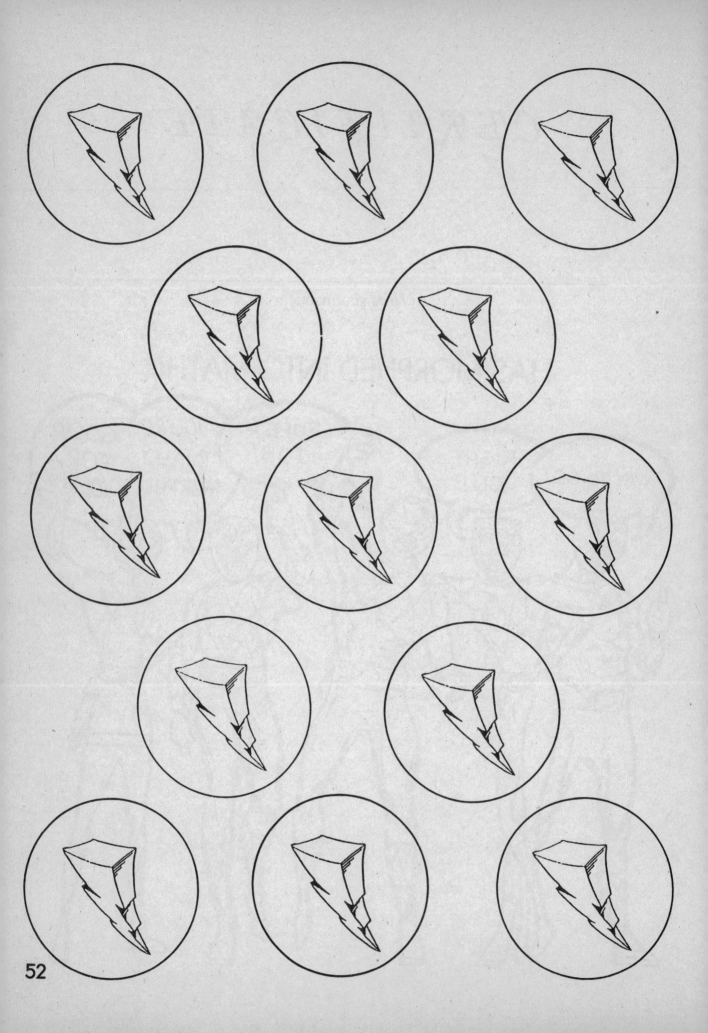

ANSWER KEY

Page 4

Page 5
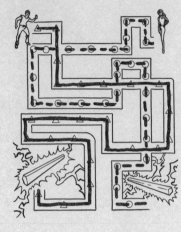

Pages 6-7

Pages 8-9
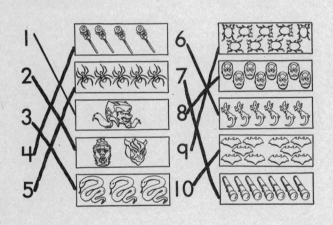

1
2
3
4
5
6
7
8
9
10

Pages 10-11

Page 12
First Row: 2, 1, 3
Second Row: 2, 3, 1
Third Row: 1, 3, 2

Page 14
5
7
3
6
4

Page 15
$1 + 1 = \boxed{2}$ P $2 + 4 = \boxed{6}$ R $3 + 1 = \boxed{4}$ T

$3 + 2 = \boxed{5}$ E $6 + 1 = \boxed{7}$ S $5 + 3 = \boxed{8}$ O

$5 + 4 = \boxed{9}$ M $8 + 2 = \boxed{10}$ L $2 + 1 = \boxed{3}$ H

L E T S
10 5 4 7

M O R P H
9 8 6 2 3

Page 16
8:00; 9:00; 10:00; 11:00; 12:00; 1:00; 2:00

Page 17

2 and 8

5 and 5

6 and 4

3 and 7

6 and 4

1 and 9

Page 18

1

4

3

2

6

Page 19

Equations that equal zero (0):

7 - 7

5 - 5

3 - 3

1 - 1

10 - 10

8 - 8

6 - 6

9 - 9

2 - 2

1 - 1

Page 20

$8 - \boxed{4} = 4$

$\boxed{9}$

$3 = 6$

$5 \ 2 = \boxed{3}$

$\boxed{6}$

$5 = 1$

$7 - \boxed{5} = 2$

$8 \ 2 = \boxed{6}$

Page 21

Red: 9 - 4; 3 + 2; 8 - 3; 5 + 0; 1 + 4; 7 - 2; 5 - 0; 6 - 1

Blue: 1 + 5; 3 + 3; 5 + 1; 8 - 2; 9 - 3; 2 + 4

Yellow: 9 - 2; 5 + 2; 6 + 1; 7 - 0; 8 - 1; 9 - 2; 1 + 6; 4 + 3; 7 + 0; 2 + 5; 8 - 1;
    7 - 0; 3 + 4

Gray: 3 + 5; 6 + 2; 8 - 0; 9 - 1

Page 22

4 + 1; 2 + 3; 5 + 0; 9 - 4; 8 - 3; 7 - 2; 6 - 1; 3 + 2; 1 + 4; 9 - 4; 8 - 3; 0 + 5

Page 23

MEET ME AT THE YOUTH CENTER.

Page 24

1	9	3	6
+4	-8	+3	-2
5	1	6	4
8	2	4	5
-5	+3	-2	+1
3	5	2	6
2	9	1	7
+2	-6	+1	-6
4	3	2	1

Page 26

S	M	T	W	T	F	S
			1	2	3	4	5
6	7	8	9	10	11	12
13	14	15	16	17	18	19
20	21	22	23	24	25	26
27	28	29	30	31		

54

Page 27

5; 10; 15; 20; 25; 30; 35; 40; 45; 50

Pages 28-29

The real Power Rangers:

2	4	8	3	7
+2	+3	+2	+2	+2
+6	+3	+0	+5	+1
10	10	10	10	10

Page 30

7	10	9		13	8	9	6	15	11
+5	+10	+9		+1	+5	+7	+5	+3	+8
12	20	18		14	13	16	11	18	19
T	H	E		N	U	M	B	E	R

12	16	9	10	7
+5	+2	+6	+8	+7
17	18	15	18	14
S	E	V	E	N

Page 31

18		19	17	18	18	16	13
-2		-1	-2	-5	-1	-4	-2
16		18	15	13	17	12	11
A		P	E	R	S	O	N

15	12		19		15	18	17	19	18
-3	-1		-3		-1	-6	-4	-2	-3
12	11		16		14	12	13	17	15
O	N		A		H	O	R	S	E

Page 32

+7	
3	10
9	16
6	13
8	15
10	17
5	12
7	14
4	11

Page 33

	-5
16	11
19	14
7	2
8	3
17	12
9	4
18	13
15	10

Page 34

56	79	67	88	95
-24	-33	-46	-31	-32
32	46	21	57	63

Page 36

5 8 1 1 6
T O M M Y

Page 38

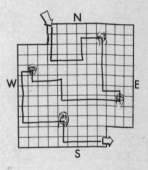

Page 39

8	19	5	20	5
[+]	[-]	[+]	[-]	[+]
7	8	3	9	9
[-]	[-]	[+]	[+]	[-]
12	6	9	3	13
=	=	=	=	=
3	5	17	14	1

Page 40

a) 49; b) 75; c) 26; d) 78; e) 13; f) 97; g) 71; h) 41; i) 99; j) 23; k) 44; l) 98; m) 37;
n) 45; o) 76; p) 15; q) 57; r) 33; s) 60; t) 21; u) 35; v) 87; w) 38; x) 61; y) 11; z) 54

Page 47

26 +32 **58**	97 -30 **67**
87 -76 **11**	21 +24 **45**
47 -14 **33**	15 +82 **97**
22 +56 **78**	79 -61 **18**

Page 49

34 +32 **66**	98 -56 **42**
65 -13 **52**	24 +15 **39**
59 -34 **25**	20 +64 **84**
44 +51 **95**	83 -11 **72**